Favorite Classics
The Adventures of
HUCKLEBERRY FINN

Retold by Sasha Morton
Illustrated by Alfredo Belli

Ticktock

An Hachette UK Company
www.hachette.co.uk

First published in the USA in 2014 by Ticktock,
an imprint of Octopus Publishing Group Ltd
Endeavour House
189 Shaftesbury Avenue
London
WC2H 8JY
www.octopusbooks.co.uk
www.octopusbooksusa.com
www.ticktockbooks.com

Distributed in the US by
Hachette Book Group USA
237 Park Avenue
New York, NY 10017, USA

Distributed in Canada by
Canadian Manda Group
165 Dufferin Street
Toronto, Ontario, Canada M6K 3H6

ISBN 978 1 84898 973 3

Printed and bound in China

10 9 8 7 6 5 4 3 2 1

Series Editor: Lucy Cuthew Design: Advocate Art
Publisher: Tim Cook Managing Editor: Karen Rigden
Production Controller: Sarah Connelly

Contents

The Characters

Iowa

Huckleberry Finn

Pap

Missouri

Texas

The
MISSISSIPPI RIVER
*Huckleberry Finn
Country*

Jim

Louisiana

Illinois

Tom Sawyer

The Duke

Jackson Island

Kentucky

Mississippi River

Arkansas

Tennessee

Mississippi

The King

Chapter 1
Huck's Plan

Once upon a time, two adventure-loving boys found buried treasure. Yes, that actually happened to me – Huckleberry Finn! Along with my good friend Tom Sawyer, I was given a $6,000 reward. That's a lot of money for a boy whose drunken father lives in prison.

After Pap went to jail, a decent lady in our town in Missouri, the Widow Douglas, adopted me and I ended up living with her and her sister, Miss Watson, and Miss Watson's slave, Big Jim.

Unfortunately, these ladies wanted me to go to school, eat my meals indoors, and become … **civilized.**

I didn't much like that.

But one night, everything changed. I went to bed and found Pap sitting right there in my room!

7

"I've been back in town two days, and all I've heard is how rich you are, boy," growled Pap.

"Give me that money or there'll be trouble!"

Now, the town judge was keeping my money safe, just in case Pap tried to get his hands on it. So Pap dragged me off to a cabin some three miles upriver, and announced he was keeping me there until the judge gave him my money.

I didn't much like being kept a prisoner, but soon I was able to spend every day fishing and climbing trees while Pap went off stealing. That meant no more school lessons, tidy hair, or clean clothes –

which suited me.

Unfortunately, Pap was mean,
and keen on beating me. So I came
up with an escape plan that would have made
my old friend Tom Sawyer proud…

I filled an old raft with supplies and hid it nearby. While Pap was out, I made the cabin look like it had been broken into and that my body had been dumped in the Mississippi River. No one would come looking for me now!

I floated silently along the riverbank in the raft. Pap himself missed me by inches as he rowed back to the cabin.

I was free!

Chapter 2
Huck and Jim

Five miles away, there was a heavily wooded, three-mile-long piece of land in the middle of the river, called Jackson's Island. It was the ideal place for a runaway to hide out, and the branches of the willow trees on its shore covered up my raft perfectly.

The next morning, I saw a ferryboat sail past, full of people looking for the body of poor Huck Finn. I even spotted good old Tom Sawyer from my hiding place!

"Keep a lookout, everyone, he might still be alive!"

called the ferry captain, but after a few more passes, they gave up the search.

After four days, I was starting to feel a bit lonesome, and so I was pleased to find company. Sound asleep near a campfire was Miss Watson's slave!

"Hello, Jim!"
I called cheerfully.

"Huck!
I thought you was dead!"
cried Big Jim.

After I explained how I came to be still alive, Jim told me, "Miss Watson sold me to a family in New Orleans! They treat their servants real mean down there, and so I want to catch a ferry to a Free State where I won't get sold again."

Now we were a pair of runaways, both of us **searching for freedom!**

For the time being, it seemed safest to stay put on Jackson's Island. We even moved our supplies into a cave that would give us good shelter as the summer storm season began.

One night, as lightning flashed and thunder roared, a wooden house floated right up to us!

Jim went in there to see what he could find.

He came out looking shaken, saying, **"Don't go inside, Huck. I've grabbed the best of what was in there."**

With that, Jim carried a trunk full of loot back to the cave, and the house floated on by.

I was curious to find out what had happened to Pap since my "murder," so I disguised myself as a girl with some clothes from the trunk and paddled to the nearby shore.

I knocked on the door of a small riverside shack, pretending to be lost. A kindly woman invited me in, and we got chatting about Huck Finn.

"At first everyone thought Huck Finn's father killed him to get all his money," sighed the woman. "Except he's gone missing, too. Big Jim is the main suspect now. He ran away the same night Huck Finn was killed."

This was not part of the plan.

And it got worse...

As I rowed back to our hideout, more of the
woman's words rang through my head.

"There's a reward of $300 for the slave and I
reckon I know where he is," she had whispered.
"I've seen smoke above Jackson's Island. My husband
is heading there at midnight to look for him..."

Scrambling into the cave,
I shook Jim awake, shouting,
"They're after us. There's no time to lose!"

We threw everything we owned onto the raft,
pushed off quickly, and floated into the darkness.

Chapter 3
On the Run

Down the great Mississippi River we went. Nobody came after us, but we'd learned our lesson about keeping out of sight and on the move.

One night, a storm blew up again. Lit by the lightning was a ruined riverboat, run aground on the rocks. Like most boys, I could never pass up an opportunity to go exploring, so I said,

"Let's land on her, Jim."

Jim reluctantly helped me
tie up the raft, and within minutes
I had scrambled aboard the dark riverboat.

I was having great fun creeping down the long corridors inside when suddenly I heard voices on the boat. I hid in a cabin until a rough group of looters had passed me by.

Just then, Jim's voice came out of the shadows whispering,

"Huck, our raft's floated away."

We were trapped on a sinking riverboat with a gang of thieves!

Through a porthole window, we could see the gang's getaway raft. It was loaded with their loot.

Quickly, we climbed aboard it and cut ourselves free, leaving the empty-handed gang stuck on the wreck far behind us. That was the last exploring I was going to do for a while!

The next stop on our journey would be in Illinois, where we would sell the riverboat loot and buy steamboat tickets to the Free States in the North. There, no one bought or sold slaves, so Jim would be saved from a life of slavery. And Pap would never find me that far away from home.

All was going to plan until, suddenly, in a thick fog, a huge steamboat loomed over us. Water pounded behind us and, with a splintering crack, we were hit!

Jim fell overboard on one side and me on the other. When I finally bobbed up in the churning waters, Jim was nowhere to be seen.

My friend was gone.

I washed up on the Kentucky side of the Mississippi River and was taken in by a decent family. Lonely weeks passed.

But one day, I was miserably exploring a swampy forest, when I could scarcely believe who I happened upon…

Jim!

"I managed to fix our raft, Huck," he told me proudly. I couldn't believe it! Within a few hours, we had set sail, but more trouble was just around the corner...

Chapter 4
The Duke and the King

They called themselves the Duke and the King, but there was nothing royal about these two men. Jim and I helped them escape from an angry mob, but as time passed, we regretted our good deed.

They were a pair of crooks.

In one town, we just about escaped with our
lives when the Duke sold tickets for a nonsense play
they didn't even perform!

The Duke and the
King perform
THE ROYAL
NONESUCH

They shared some of the money they made with us, but Jim
and I were desperate to get free of them. We were sure they
were planning even worse schemes, and we didn't want anything
to do with them.

No matter how we tried to shake them off, the Duke and the King kept taking charge of the raft. Days passed, and we headed further south down the river.
Our captors were plotting something devious, and Jim and I were worried…

We were right. While they were running errands, the Duke and the King sold Jim for $30 to a local family called the Phelpses. Mr. and Mrs. Phelps knew there was a $300 reward for finding Jim and intended to claim it.

Luckily, I had hidden the raft from the Duke and the King, so I got away.

I had to head to the Phelpses' cotton plantation and get Jim back,

before he was lost forever.

I moored the raft and began the long, hot walk up to their house.

Just then, a wagon rolled past me, and sitting in the back of it was none other than my old friend, **Tom Sawyer!**

"Huck Finn!" he cried. "I thought you were murdered!"

Hopping up alongside him, I explained that I was on a rescue mission. I found out that Tom was paying a long overdue visit to his aunt and uncle, who were none other than Silas and Sally Phelps, the very folks who'd bought Jim!

Tom rubbed his hands with glee at the thought of a new adventure and declared, **"I'll help you steal Jim back!"**

Chapter 5
Huck and Tom

"Why, Tom, it's been years since we saw you!" Aunt Sally smiled at me. Part of Tom's elaborate plan to free Big Jim was for me to pretend to be Tom Sawyer.

Tom was pretending to be his own half-brother, Sid, to account for there being two boys visiting the Phelps family instead of one. Aunt Sally and Uncle Silas couldn't have been more welcoming, which made what we were about to do seem even worse…

"Tom, let's just steal your uncle's keys when he's asleep, get Jim out of his cabin, and escape on my raft," I suggested.

"What's the good of a plan if it ain't more trouble than that, Huck?!" replied an exasperated Tom. "We'll dig him out with tools we make ourselves. It'll only take a week!"

Once Tom had come up with a plan, nobody could change his mind about it. In fact, Tom had us making rope ladders and digging an escape tunnel with a spoon – he even considered sawing Jim's leg off to make his escape look more convincing!

The night of Jim's breakout finally came around. To add to the adventure, Tom had sent the Phelpses a note tipping them off!

Mr. Phelps

A gang of cut-throats are planning to steal your runaway slave at midnight tonight!

Be ready.

An unknown friend

That night, while men with rifles protected the farmhouse, Tom and I slithered into Jim's cabin through our carefully dug tunnel.

Jim was wearing one of Aunt Sally's dresses, as Tom had instructed, so scrambling through the tunnel was hard going for him.

Soon, though, we were climbing the fence that led to the river and our precious raft.

Just then, a branch under Tom's foot snapped, and a voice yelled,

"Who's that?"

followed by the sound of gunfire.

Stumbling, tripping, and staggering,

we ran to the raft and pushed off into the water. It was only then that we realized Tom Sawyer had been shot when the men gave chase!

"I'll stay with Mister Tom, Huck," said Jim. "You go get the doctor."

"No Jim! You'll be captured again, and you'll never be a free man!" I fretted.

But Jim wouldn't have it any other way, and Tom was in too much pain to argue.

Before long, Tom's wounded leg had been bandaged, and Jim was back in his cabin, waiting for his owners to collect him.

44

Everything had gone wrong...

It got worse. A few days later, Tom's Aunt Polly came to visit. She knew right away that I was not Tom Sawyer and Tom Sawyer was not Sid.

The game was up!

None of this bothered Tom Sawyer, of course. Cheerfully, he explained the whole plan to the Phelps family and his Aunt Polly. He had a surprise for me, too.

"Huck, guess what?" Tom announced. "The Duke and the King got arrested, so they won't bother you any more. And Miss Watson died two months ago and set Jim free in her will! He doesn't have to be a slave any more."

I was astonished!

46

All this time, Tom could have just told his uncle to set Jim free, but no, he had to have an adventure! Jim was mighty delighted about his freedom, but what would become of me?

"Huck, your pa's dead," Jim told me sadly.
"I saw his body in that house that floated
past us in the storm on Jackson's Island."

"But the judge kept your $6,000 safe from Pap
after you "died," interrupted Tom.

"You're a rich orphan, Huck!"

With that, I decided to rebuild the raft and head on out West.
Tom's Aunt Sally is talking about adopting me and making
me civilized. I can't do that. I've tried it before – and I know it
won't work out well!